# What She Didn't Know

## By: Chris Siggers

Copyright © 2021 Chris Siggers

All rights reserved. This book is a work of fiction. Names, characters, places, and incidents either are the product of the author's imagination or are used fictitiously and are not to be construed as real. Any resemblance to actual persons, living or dead, business establishments, events, or locales or, is entirely coincidental.

No portion of this book may be used or reproduced in any manner whatsoever without writer permission except in the case of brief quotations embodied in critical articles and reviews.

# Table of Contents

**Chapter 1: A Fresh Start** ...... 1
**Chapter 2: Strange Events** ...... 10
**Chapter 3: The Perfect Guy** ...... 25
**Chapter 4: Moving Fast** ...... 34
**Chapter 5: Things Start To Heat Up** ...... 42
**Chapter 6: The Set-Up** ...... 47
**Chapter 7: Behind Bars** ...... 54
**Chapter 8: Strange Behavior** ...... 65
**Chapter 9: Saving Carli** ...... 74

Sarah Harrington is single, divorced, and new to the state of Florida. Finding the man of her dreams should be the icing on the cake, but will this romance turn into a nightmare?

※ ※ ※

## Chapter 1: A Fresh Start

"We're here, kiddos!" Sarah yelled as she and her children entered the new state of Florida.

It's so beautiful here. Sarah Harrington, a single, divorced mom, was driving her 2018 Black GMC terrain. She's a thirty-nine-year-old Caucasian with black hair. She has two children, a six-year-old daughter Carli, and a nine-year-old Zack. Sarah and the children's father decided to get a divorce six months ago, and she's been working two jobs trying to support her children. She decided after her divorce to leave North Carolina and move to Florida to start a new life for her and her children.

Sarah had always wanted to leave Carolina, but she loved her job there and bonded with her coworkers. Sarah was a nurse, and she loves what she does. She also worked at a hotel on weekends doing housekeeping to bring in extra money in the house. Sarah had felt her life was very ordinary, so she planned to move to Florida, which is where she has always wanted to go. She started looking for nursing jobs here, and she then started searching for homes.

Although it was just her now and the cost of living would be a lot higher here, Sarah decides to step out on faith and make that move anyhow.

"Oh wow, mom! It's so cool here," Carli comments.

"I know, baby girl, it's incredible."

Sarah drives through the beautiful neighborhood and begins to cry.

"What's wrong, mommy?" Carli asked. She's always been a mommy's girl. Zack on the other hand he wants to be with his dad.

"Nothing, hunni, everything is okay now."

The neighborhood is filled with huge, nice homes. There are enormous trees in front of the yards and seems to be a swimming pool in every backyard. Sarah and her children pull into the driveway, and they noticed some boys throwing a football in their front yard. As the vehicle stops, Zack jumps out of the truck. "Yes! Bye, mom!"

"Zack, be in before dark." Zack is a huge football fan. He wants to become a professional athlete when he grows up.

Sarah and Carli get out of the car and walks into the house.

"Wow, this is so beautiful!" Sarah comments as she walks around the living room.

This house was stunning! It was a three-bedroom house. The rooms were huge with large walk-in closets, a fireplace in the living room, the dining area was huge, and the kitchen has a nice bar in the middle with marble countertops. Everything was perfect. Sarah had already fallen in love with this house.

"Can we pick out my room now?" Carli asks as she grabs her mom by the hand and runs up the stairs.

As they tour the rest of the house, they hear a knock at the door. As Sarah runs downstairs to open the door, she notices a tall, Caucasian, gorgeous man standing there. This man had to be specially made by God. His skin was smooth, his black hair was silky, and his facial hair was connected just right.

Sarah stood there a few seconds admiring his beauty before she finally says, "Can I help you?"

The man smiles and says, "Actually, I was taking my trash out and noticed you still had your keys in the door. I live right next door."

"Ooh, how silly of me, thank you so much. What is your name?"

"I'm Connor Gibson." He shakes her hand and then asks for her name.

"I'm Sarah Harrington."

They lock eyes for about two seconds, and then Sarah says, "Well, thank you, Connor, and it was nice to meet you."

"Likewise," Connor replies. "Sooo, is it you and your husband or just you?"

# What She Didn't Know

"It's just me. I'm divorced." Connor gives another sexy stare. "Well again, it was nice meeting you, and thanks for noticing the keys."

As Sarah tries to close the door, Connor sticks his feet out and stops the door. "Okay, I'm so embarrassed at what I'm about to say, but you're so beautiful, and I would love to take you to dinner tonight."

Sarah hasn't been on a date in over six months, and she hasn't been around another man either. As bad as she wants to say yes to the date, she turns him down.

"I'm sorry, Conner, but I don't think that would be a good idea right now. I just got the divorce finalized, and I'm not ready to date just yet. Of course, she hates herself for what she just did, but somehow, she's trying to act 'uninterested'.

"I understand, bad timing. Just know I'm waiting for you." Connor was willing to wait for Sarah. He has never met anyone like her before.

*** *** ***

A few weeks later, Sarah goes out for a run through the neighborhood. She always made sure to keep herself fit, and jogging was her hobby. She's halfway down the road, and suddenly she hears a familiar voice.

"You're pretty fast there. I'm not sure I can keep up." It was Connor. He's desperately trying to get with Sarah, so he's willing to do whatever it takes just to be around her.

"Oh, hey, Connor, right?" Sarah says while taking her earbuds out of her ear.

Connor smiles as he continues the small talk, "You remembered. I'm flattered."

Sarah tries to keep her composure since she thinks he's so hot, but she doesn't want him to think she is interested.

"I'm good at remembering names. So, you're following me now?"

Of course, Sarah wants him to follow her. This was the man she's been thinking about for the last few weeks. She definitely playing hard to get.

"Nah, just getting a little run in before bed. This body isn't going to keep itself up, you know. So, what made you move out here?"

"It was time for a new start for the kids and me. I think this is going to be a great place for us."

Connor smiles. That was exactly what he wanted to hear. "Well, if you ever want to take a break from mom world and get out and have a nice evening, I would love to accommodate you."

## What She Didn't Know

Sarah smiles and tells him she'll keep that in mind. However, deep down inside, she was dying to spend the evening with Connor.

"Well, I'll let you continue your run. I'll see you later, hopefully."

Sarah puts her earbuds back in and smiles from ear-to-ear as she continues her run. Connor could be the one for Sarah. Although she doesn't know much about him, yet she may have met the man of her dreams.

Sarah and her ex-husband argued a lot. They never seemed to agree on anything. Ethan had a drinking problem. When he would get drunk, he would get furious. Although he never hit her, he destroys their home by breaking things when they would fight. Carli would cry because she was scared, but Zack wasn't afraid of his father. Zack and his father were remarkably close. No matter what Ethan did, Zack took up for him. He was a daddy's boy. Zack is still mad at Sarah for divorcing his dad, and he has temper tantrums from time to time.

One time she and Zack had an argument, and he ran away. He didn't come home for two days. Sarah always tried to make excuses for him when we behave that way, but truth be told, she needed to grab a belt and whoop his backside.

Sarah never disciplined her children by whooping them. She didn't believe in that. Instead, she would take their video games and make them go to their room. It's time for church, Carli yells as she comes into her mom's room.

"Oh, thanks, baby girl, but mommy is tired today, no church this morning. Where is your brother?"

"He's next door with some, man," Carli says.

Sarah rushes downstairs and goes outdoors and sees Zack throwing the football with Connor.

"Well, good morning, beautiful. I hope we didn't wake you," Connor greets as he throws the ball to Zack.

"Oh no, you're fine. Zack didn't bother you, did he?" Sarah has this annoyed look on her face.

"Not at all, he just asked to play a little catch, so I didn't mind."

"Ok, well, Zack, I'm about to start on breakfast, so come inside and wash your hands," Sarah advises as she tries not to pay any attention to Connor.

"I noticed your landscaping needed some work. I could do it for you at no charge."

"What do you mean? Do it for me?"

"I'm a landscaper. My father and I started our own company years ago, and after he died, I took over."

"Oh, sorry to hear about your father," Sarah offers her condolences.

"It's okay. He lived a long life. So, would you be up to me helping you?"

"And you're willing to do it for free? I'm sorry I can't do that. What is your fee?"

"I can't take your money, but I would love to take you to dinner instead."

Sarah puts her head down and smiles. "You just don't give up, do you?"

"Not until I get what I want," Connor says.

"Okay. It's a date."

"Friday at seven o'clock. See you later."

* * *

Later that night, at dinner, Sarah asked Zack what he thought of Connor.

"He's okay, I guess," Zack answered.

Carli tries to pour another glass of tea and spills it on the table. "Sorry, mom."

"It's okay. I got it," Sarah says as she continues to talk to Zack. "He's got to be more than just okay if you asked him to throw the football with you.

"I didn't ask him. He asked me," Zack says as he cleans his plate.

"He asked you. I thought he said you asked him?" Sarah replies as she has a strange look on her face.

"No, he saw me in the yard and asked could he join me."

That had to be a little strange for Zack, because he rarely opens up to anyone that easily. Maybe Connor bribed him with something. Or maybe Zack is trying to open up more and face the reality that his parents aren't getting back together, so his dad isn't going to be around as much as he would want him to.

"When did you decide to be so nice to strangers?" Sarah asks.

"I didn't really think about it, he asked, and I just went for it," Zack replies.

Moving to a new state can be tough for small children. Zack and Carli will eventually meet new friends and really get settled into the new lifestyle. Florida was different. It is so much for the kids to do here, even though they may just end up at the beach most of their time since they love the water.

When they were smaller, they went to the beach, and Zack almost drowned. This was one of the worst moments in Sarah's life. They turned their backs for two minutes, and there he was going under. You would think that would scare Zack off going back near the water, but he still loves it. The children have always had a great childhood growing up. Sarah and Ethan would always take them on trips every summer whenever they weren't involved with other summer activities. They seemed to have it all, and now this new life would be perfect for them.

## Chapter 2: Strange Events

*"The time now is 9:45, and your local Walgreens will close in fifteen minutes. Please bring all items to the front register for a speedy and courtesy checkout. Walgreens will open at 8:00 a.m. tomorrow morning. Thanks again for shopping at Walgreens."*

Sarah tries to hurry and grab her final items before heading to the checkout. Tonight she's making cheeseburgers for the kids. She hasn't cooked in a while. They usually eat out a lot. As she gets to the counter, a woman grabs her basket.

"BE CAREFUL, BE VERY CAREFUL!" warns a very elderly Caucasian woman who looks to be in her late 70s.

Sarah is afraid of what the woman said because she looked as she had terror in her eyes. Sarah doesn't say a word as she watches the lady walk out of the store. This was very creepy. Sarah has never seen this woman in her life and grabbing her basket saying crazy things was very strange.

When Sarah finished shopping, she headed to the truck and noticed the old woman sitting in a black van starting at her.

"What is her problem?" Sarah quizzes as she tries to hurry and put her grocery in the back seat.

The old woman doesn't say a word. She just sits there. Who knows, the woman may actually have a mental problem, or could it be that she has Sarah confused with someone else. Either way, it's definitely shaken Sarah's nerves up.

* * *

Sarah lays in her bed, thinking about what the lady has told her. She stayed up all night trying to figure out why this lady whom she doesn't know would tell her something like that. This was very strange. While reading a book, she receives a call from her friend Valerie.

"Hey, girl? What are you doing?"

"Hey Val, I'm sitting here reading a book and waiting on some cookies to get done."

"Are you still reading *What's Love without a Tragedy?*

"Yes. It's so good. I'm almost at the end. Authoress Rayven is incredible. You should definitely get a copy."

"Yes, maybe, I should. I'll order a copy tomorrow after work. Sooooo, are you excited about Friday night?"

"What's happening Friday night?"

"Oh Sarah please, you know you haven't stopped thinking about Connor and this date Friday night so don't even try it, missy."

"I guess I'm excited, I mean what will I wear?

"I'm sure you can find something in that closet. You just bought a lot of new clothes that you haven't worn, so this would be the perfect time to wear them. Maybe a dress, nice sexy dress. Black dress...no, red dress. Hell, I don't know I'm just as excited as you are. He could be THE ONE!"

"The one would be nice, but I definitely need to know more about him first."

"Of course, and Friday night is the perfect night to do so."

"We'll see. This will be my first date since the divorce and I'm just nervous about the whole thing.". What if he's crazy, what if he's married or gay? I just..."

"Sarah, stop! Conner's perfect. You'll see."

"For my kids' sake, I hope so. They really could use a father figure in their life."

"You need to put Ethan on child support," Valerie advises.

"No, Ethan takes care of the kids, and I can't take that away from him, but he just wasn't around like he should have been. He's missed so many games this year and let's not mention school meetings. I've had it up to here with Ethan, but I'm hoping he changes."

"I hope so too so that he can get that bond back with the kids.

"If he doesn't want another man raising his kids, he had better get on the ball," Valerie says as she sips her champagne.

"Well enough about him, I'm ready to see what Connor is all about," Sarah changes the subject as she plays in her hair.

"I'm sure he's fine… and I'm not just talking about his looks."

"Well, why not? The looks are to die for, hunni."

"Are you gonna have sex with him?

"Uhh, nooo! I barely know him. He's gotta work hard for the cookies… and even then, I'm not gonna give it up so quick."

"Whatever hunni, you say that now, but talk to me in a couple of weeks, Valerie comments.

"Whatever, we will see. I'm gonna get some sleep. I'll call you tomorrow to finish this conversation."

*** *** ***

Sarah goes for a ride one night with the kids downtown to check out the scenery.

"It's so cool here, mom," Carli expresses as she's looking out the window admiring the beautiful buildings.

"Zack, what do you think about the city?"

"It's okay, I guess. I just wish dad were here to enjoy it with us."

Zack has been acting differently ever since the move. He's not actually excited about moving here without his dad and wishes things could go back to being normal. Sarah tries every day to get him to like the new move, but it's challenging getting him to accept the change. Maybe Ethan should move there and get a separate place to be there for the kids? Then again, that wouldn't work because Sarah's new man wouldn't stand a chance. Ethan would try his best to destroy that relationship before it even starts.

After Sarah and Ethan's divorce, Sarah tried to inform him that eventually, she will find someone else and that man would have to be around the kids. Ethan didn't like that and suggested that she waited a year or two before she started seeing someone. Of course, Sarah didn't agree to wait an entire year before getting involved with someone. I mean, who could do that, especially when it's his fault that the marriage is over. Ethan should have been focused on saving his marriage rather than turning to an alcohol bottle and staying out all night at bars.

They say you don't miss a good thing until it's gone, and in this case, that's exactly what's happening. Every other day Ethan calls and tries to get back with Sarah, but Sarah doesn't fall for it because she knows that it's just him talking a good talk for now, and later going back to his old ways. Sarah wanted better. She wanted better for her children. She wanted a man who respected her, and valued her, and didn't drink all day and night. She wanted someone who she could be at peace with and not argue daily. Connor could be that guy, but in due time she will find out so.

Sarah stops by a fast food restaurant and grabs them some burgers. After she orders their food, she noticed a strange young woman in all black staring at her two cars behind in the drive thru. This was very creepy. The lady didn't even turn her head when she noticed Sarah caught her staring. She just kept looking as if something was wrong with her.

*What the heck is her problem?* Sarah thought to herself.

Sarah pays for the food, grabs her order, and pulls off quickly, trying to get out of the drive-thru and away from the lady. As she's driving down the road, she keeps thinking about the woman and why was she staring at her. Things have definitely been strange since she moved here.

*** *** ***

The next night she stops by the gas station and stands in line to pay for her gas. The guy in front of her drops his money on the ground, so Sarah brings it to his attention.

"Sir, you dropped your money."

The guy thanks her, and before she could say another word, she notices the same old lady again. This was the strange lady who told her to be very careful a few weeks ago. Sarah tries to hurry and pay for her gas without talking to her. As she's rushing to pump the gas, she texts her friend Valerie.

**Sarah:** *Hey, are you busy? I need to talk to you.*

Before Sarah could send the text, the lady grabs her on her arm and says, "He's dangerous, extremely dangerous. Stay away!"

Sarah doesn't even finish pumping her gas. She hangs the pump up and quickly gets in the truck and drives off fast. At this point, she's afraid of what's going on, so she gives Valerie a call.

"Hey, hunni, what's up?" Valerie greets.

"Valerie, this strange, old lady has been following me and telling me things. I don't know who she is and what she wants."

"Okay, call down, Sarah. Now, who is following you?"

"A few weeks ago, I went to the store, and this lady came to me saying 'be careful', and now at the gas station she comes up to me again telling me 'he's dangerous'. Valerie, I've never seen this woman in my life, and I have no idea what she's talking about."

"Oh wow, have you called the police?"

"I can't call the police because she hasn't physically done anything to me. She's just scaring me.

"Wow! You need to keep your mace on you at all times, but I'm sure it's nothing too serious."

"Nothing too serious??? This woman is clearly stalking me, and I'm not even sure why."

"Sarah, calm down. She probably has Alzheimer's and doesn't even know what she's doing.

"I hope so because she's very creepy, and it's scaring me."

## What She Didn't Know

As Sarah pulls into the driveway, she notices she didn't even get all of her gas. This lady has terrified her. She sits in the truck for a few minutes, trying to calm down. As she messes with her phone, she looks up, and there's Connor.

"Oh my god! You scared me."

"I'm sorry I didn't mean to scare you," Connor says.

"How long have you been standing there?" Sarah quizzes with a strange look on her face.

"Not long. I just noticed you looked worried, like something had scared you."

"Oh, I'm fine, it's nothing. Thanks for being concerned."

"It's my pleasure," Connor comments as he goes back into his house.

*** *** ***

Friday, May 9, 2018, Sarah gets ready for her date with Connor. This is the moment she's been waiting for a while now. She's so nervous, and to calm herself down, she takes a shot.

"He could be the one," " Valerie encourages, as she grabs the bottle of champagne from Sarah.

"I don't know. How I look?"

"Girl, you're fine, relax.

"I just want this to be perfect. I haven't dated in forever, and Conner is so hot!"

"Sarah, everything will be fine, trust me, just remember to not talk so much and try not to be on your phone. It's rude.

"Okay, he's here. Don't forget to lock up, and thanks again for watching the kids. I owe you.

*** *** ***

Connor and Sarah are at Deluxious, a fancy restaurant in downtown Florida. She is wearing a black, silky dress and silver shoes. She has a beautiful necklace, and her diamond earrings are sparking. Connor is well dressed himself wearing gray dress pants with a blue collared shirt. His cologne has to be the best smelling cologne a man could wear.

"You look so beautiful," Connor says as he pulls out the chair for Sarah.

"Thank you. You look ok yourself."

Sarah knew Connor was fine as hell, but of course, she couldn't say that.

"You come here often?" Sarah asks as she looks through the menu to order.

"No. It's actually my first time coming to this place. I heard through a friend that the food is fantastic."

"Well, it's a beautiful place. Everyone looks amazing, and it's tranquil."

"Not used to peace, I'm guessing."

"No, it's just... well, where I'm from, it's always busy."

"Well, maybe it's time to change that."

In the middle of the conversation, a woman walks up to the table and screams, "WHAT ARE YOU DOING HERE? YOU'RE NOT SUPPOSED TO BE HERE! WHY ARE YOU HERE???"

The woman is screaming loud and scaring Sarah.

As the owner escorts her out, the woman says to Sarah, "RUN! HE'S DANGEROUS.... IF I WERE YOU, I WOULD RUN NOW AND WATCH YOUR BACK!"

Sarah and Connor jump up from the table as the server comes over and tries to calm things down. "I'm so sorry! Please don't go. We are taking care of that situation, and she won't bother you all again."

"Who was that, and why was she calling you Peter Collins?"

"I have no idea," Connor answers. "I think she's on something. I've never seen that woman before in my life."

"She acted as if she knew you, Connor."

"Sarah, sweetie, listen. I can assure you that I've never met that woman — EVER. She must have me confused with someone else."

Sarah has a confused look on her face. She's so upset and scared that she doesn't know what to do, so she goes to the ladies' room and gets herself together.

Starting in the mirror, "What just happened?" she voices to her reflection. "Why was she calling Connor Peter Collins?"

*** *** ***

Later that night, Sarah sits in her bed, thinking about what happened earlier. That was scary. Nothing like that has ever happened to Sarah before. While watching television, she receives a text from Connor.

**Connor:** *I'm sorry about tonight. Things got a little crazy, but I really enjoyed you. Looking forward to taking you out again sometime."*

Although everything went crazy, Sarah is still open to going out with Connor again. Sarah doesn't respond right away because she can't help but think, *what's going on?* That was strange, and she had never dealt with anything like this before. She likes Connor, but she doesn't want to move too fast, and he turns out to be crazy. Sarah was always taught to never listen to anyone and always stick by your man, but Connor wasn't her man yet. If this woman is making these allegations, then Sarah certainly wants to make sure she's making the right decision by continuing to go out with him.

*** *** ***

A few weeks later, while picking the kids up from school, Sarah makes a quick stop by the deli. While grabbing her things, she receives a strange phone call.

"HE'S NOT WHO HE SAYS HE IS!"

"Hello…who is this? Hello!"

Something was definitely up. Sarah hasn't given her number out to anyone since she's been in the state. The calls come in every few days saying something different. *Who could this be?* she wondered. Things were getting stranger by the weeks. One night she went out to her car, and there was a note attached to her driver's side door handle.

The note read: *PETER COLLINS!!!!!*

Peter Collins?? Sarah wondered who that could be and why was a note attached to her door handle. She never told anyone about the things that have been happening other than the strange old lady she told Valerie about. She didn't want to freak anyone out.

*** *** ***

One Friday evening, she went on a run. Sarah hadn't run in a while, and she needed to get back in the game.

Connor drives past." How's it going?

"Oh, hey. It's going good. I'm just getting my run in. How about yourself?"

"I couldn't be better now that I've seen you."

"I'm flattered, but where are you headed?"

"Oh, headed to town to get some things. What are you doing tomorrow night?"

"As of now, I don't have any plans."

I'm cooking at my place, and I would love to invite you over."

"Okay, sure...what time?"

"Dinner will be ready at eight o'clock. See you there."

*This is my second chance to be with this guy,* Sarah thought to herself as she continued her run. Connor was looking hotter day by day. He was just so fine. Sarah just had to accept the dinner offer and spend another romantic night with Connor.

*** *** ***

It's Friday, and Sarah heads over to Connor. *I hope I'm not moving too fast...* she thought to herself... *what if he thinks I'm easy?*"

Sarah arrives at Connor's place and rings the doorbell.

"Well, hello, beautiful. May I say you look more and more stunning by the day?"

Sarah blushes and says, "Thank you, you don't look too bad yourself."

As she walks in, she notices the dinner table was already set.

"This is beautiful, Connor."

"Not as beautiful as you," he compliments while pulling her chair out.

An hour passes and she pulls out her phone and sends a text to Valerie.

**Sarah:** *Hey, just checking on you and the kids. I'll be home in a few hours.*

**Valerie:** *Girl, don't worry about us, enjoy your new man, hunni and take your time. We are watching a movie.*

'Who's taking your attention away from me?" Connor asks while pouring her a glass of wine.

"Oh, I was just texting my friend Valerie."

Connor smiles as he moves his chair closer to her. "So... are you enjoying yourself?"

"Yes. I definitely am. Are you?" Sarah counters.

Connor puts the glass of wine down and gently rubs his hands on Sarah's face. "Let me show you how much I am."

Connor kisses her slowly. His lips were smooth and soft. He kissed Sarah as if she were the last woman on earth. He then picks her up with her legs wrapped around his waist... lays her on the couch and begins to make love to her. He made love to her in ways she has never imagined, and it was the best sex she ever had.

# Chapter 3: The Perfect Guy

While taking a walk in the park, Sarah calls Valerie.

"Hey, Sarah."

"Hey Val, got a minute?"

"Yeah, sure, what's up?"

"Hey, I wanted to talk to you about Connor."

"You mean your new husband... sure," Valarie comments, laughing.

"You're so funny, but this is serious. So, Connor and I have gotten remarkably close lately, and everything is perfect. Well, almost perfect."

"What do you mean, almost Sarah? What did the man do?"

"Well, we've been spending a lot of time together, but I've been getting strange calls from unknown numbers and with the woman at the restaurant... I don't know, things just seem strange."

"Oh, Sarah, I'm sure it's nothing. He said he didn't know the woman at the restaurant, right?"

"Yeah."

"Well, I don't think you have anything to worry about... Just give him a chance."

"I don't know."

"Sarah, please stop doing that."

"Doing what?"

"Trying to ruin the only chance you have with this amazing fine man."

"Excuse me?"

"Look, I'm just saying…"

"I cannot believe you! How dare you say that to me?"

"Sarah, you're getting carried away. Just calm down.

"No, let me tell you something. I'm not perfect. I'm far from it, but I will not date someone who may be hiding something. That's just not who I am. I'll call you later. I got to go.

Sarah furious with Valerie. She cannot believe Valerie is trying to say she's about to ruin this just because she has her suspicions about Connor. Connor was attractive — extremely attractive — but it's not enough to become blind to unusual things occurring.

*** *** ***

It's 7:30, and the kids are doing homework. Sarah pours herself a bottle of wine and watches television. While watching, she noticed she didn't finish putting up her curtains, so she goes over to the curtains, and while putting them up, she notices that her door is unlocked. Sarah clearly remembers locking the door but thinks maybe one of the kids unlocked it by mistake. After putting up the curtains, she heads to bed.

*** *** ***

The next day everyone heads to the car to go shopping. It's Saturday. Everything was on sale today at nearby stores, and Sarah just had to get up and go catch a few. As she and the kids get in the car, she notices a strange woman driving by her house. The woman was driving a black van, and she looks like she's had a rough life. The woman drives by slowly, then she stops.

"Hey... can I help you?" Sarah says as she hurries to get the kids in the truck.

The woman doesn't say a word. She just stares.

"Are you looking for someone?"

The woman suddenly drives off really fast.

Sarah is completely freaked out and has seen nothing like this before. *Who could this woman be?* She thought as she got into her truck and pulled out the driveway.

While walking around the store, she called Valerie.

"Hey ... are you free?"

"So now you want to talk to me?

"I'm sorry, Val, I was just going through some things."

"Is everything okay?"

"Well, I'm not sure. I was leaving the house today, and this strange woman drove by looking very creepy, and she stopped the car and just stared at me."

"Oh, wow! Have you ever seen her before?

"No. I have no idea what she wanted and why she was acting so weird."

"I'm starting to worry."

"Have you talked to Connor?"

"No. I don't want to worry him with all of this and speaking of Connor. I have something to tell you ..."

"Ohhhhh, let me pour a glass for this one."

"Connor and I had sex!"

"Shut uppppp! Sarah, are you serious?" Valerie quizzed delightfully. "Wait, a minute. You're not playing with me, right? Is this another one of your jokes?"

"No. We had sex, and it was AMAZING! I've never had anything like that before, and I definitely want it again!" Sarah gushes.

"Oh my god, my sweet Sarah has been turned out by this gorgeous man! So what is the next step for you guys? When am I going to meet him?"

## What She Didn't Know

"Soon. I just want to make sure he's the one first.... you know how that is."

Sarah was blushing about this man. She's never felt this way about anyone before. Could Connor be the man she's been waiting on?

"Well, you guys need to hurry up and get things figured out. I have trips for us to take as couples. Does he have any children?" Valerie probes.

"No children. Conner's always wanted them, but his work never let him have the time.

Well, he has two bad rugrats now to deal with. I'm sure Zack and Carli will keep him on his toes.

"Oh, Lord, let's pray not. I think they like him. Zack is always throwing the football with him, so I really think he likes him just a tad bit, Carli hasn't been around him much, but you know her, she will love him!" Well, what about your parents? Have you told them about Connor?"

No, not yet, but I'm going to tell them soon. You know how mom is. She's been trying to get me to date since the divorce, and Dad has as well," Sarah reveals.

"Well, what are you waiting on, missy? Tell them!" Valerie encourages.

"I will... just waiting for the right moment.

Sarah's parents never liked Zack and Carli's father, Ethan. They always told Sarah that he wasn't good for her and that she needed to find someone else. One night during an argument at her parents' house, Ethan threw a lamp and stormed out the door. They just never respected him after that, even after his fake apology. They would be thrilled to learn that Sarah has a new man in her life, but she first has to make sure he's the one!

*** *** ***

Connor and Sarah have lunch at this amazing place in downtown Florida. They checked out this new place, and since the summer just started, the kids were out of school and gone away to camp. While talking to Connor and laughing at his jokes, Sarah notices a scratch on his neck, and it was bleeding.

"Connor, you're bleeding! What happened to your neck?"

"Oh it's nothing. I scratched it this morning, fooling around with my cat. Her name is Bella, and she's always scratching me up," Connor replied.

"So, tell me a little more about you," Sarah requests as she sips her wine.

"Well, I'm from California, my parents died, and I've never had children. I've always wanted children, but I never met the right one, so I decided to get a cat instead."

# What She Didn't Know

"I'm allergic to cats, by the way," Sarah discloses while smiling and putting her hands over her mouth, "but I'm sure you'll keep her away from me while I'm over at your place."

"Of course I will... anything for you! So are you enjoying yourself with me so far?" Conner asks.

"I am. I haven't felt this way in a long time, and I'm not sure if I know how to date anymore... but I'm working on that."

"Well, you're doing just fine. Just let me take care of you."

*** *** ***

Later that night, Sarah stops by the gym to workout. While running on the treadmill, she glances at the television and sees that they had reported a local woman missing earlier this morning. Sarah stops running. It's the woman from the restaurant. This was the woman who came up to the table, causing a scene about Connor and calling him Peter Collins. This is horrible. Sarah calls Valerie...

"Hey Val, got a minute?"

"Yeah, what's up?"

"Hey, you know that woman I told you about that was at the restaurant a few weeks ago who acted strange with Connor and me?"

"Yes, I remember."

"Valerie, she's missing."

"What????"

"I'm watching the news now. They say she was scheduled to work and never showed. Oh, God, that's terrible.

"Yeah, it is... but I'm at the gym. I was just wanting to let you know that. I'll call you tomorrow and discuss our plans for this weekend."

*** *** ***

As Sarah drives home, she can't help but think about the woman being missing. She texts Connor.

**Sarah:** *Hey, are you up?*

**Connor:** *Yes, I am. What's up?*

**Sarah:** *Hey, I was just watching the news, and the woman who harassed us at the restaurant a few weeks ago was reported missing this morning!*

**Connor:** *Oh, wow, are you serious?*

**Sarah:** *Yes. It's so crazy life is truly something, here one minute, the next you're gone.*

**Connor:** *I hate that, but are you free this weekend?*

**Sarah:** *I guess you're right! And I have plans with Valerie this weekend.*

**Connor:** *I'm sure you can find a good reason to cancel.*

**Sarah:** *You want me to cancel on my best friend?*

**Connor:** *You'll be happy you did. Trust me. I have something special for you.*

Sarah takes a deep breath and thinks it over.

**Sarah:** *Okay. I'll just tell her something came up, but this better be good That's my girl.*

**Connor:** *Well, I gotta go. You get some rest.*

# Chapter 4: Moving Fast

*Waking up in a new house with no kids around is wonderful,* Sarah thought to herself. Even though the kids are only going to be gone for a month, this was definitely some alone time. Since moving to Florida, Sarah hasn't found a nursing job, so she decided to teach at an elementary school for the time being. Today she caught up on her assignments for the summer school program, which she teaches this summer. Her students love her, but some of them can be a handful.

After a few hours of making lesson plans for her students, she goes to a spa and treats herself for a change. As she leaves the house, she notices Connor is behind her.

"Hey, are you following me?"

"No," Connor says. I'm just making sure you're safe."

"Making sure I'm safe? I think I can handle myself."

"I'm sure you can, but why should you?" Connor looks at Sarah as if she were the only woman on earth. He wanted her so bad. "What are your plans for today?"

"Well, I'm going to the spa later, and after I'm going to catch a movie. Why?"

"Just asking, mind if I join?"

This was strange. Sarah wanted some alone time and here comes Connor requesting to go to the spa with her. She's already seeing him this weekend, and she begins to think he's too clingy.

"Sure, why not? I have to go to the store and grab some things, do I'll text you the address to the spa."

\* \* \*

While at the spa, Connor goes and orders some wine for them, and while he's gone, Sarah is approached by a nice-looking man.

"Hey, I've never seen any beautiful women around here. You're definitely the first."

"Well, thank you," says Sarah while trying to ignore him but smiles and plays it off.

"Would you mind if I joined you?"

"Well, I'm with…"

Before she could get another word out, Connor comes over and grabs him by the neck.

"IF YOU WANNA KEEP YOUR TONGUE, I SUGGEST YOU BACK OFF! OTHERWISE, I'LL RIP IT RIGHT OUT OF YOUR MOUTH!"

"CONNOR… STOP!" Sarah urged.

Connor was freaking out. He had totally lost and when he saw that someone was talking to Sarah and the crazy part is that they haven't been a couple very long and he's already moving fast.

"YOU GET AWAY FROM AROUND HERE! DON'T EVER LET ME CATCH YOU TALKING TO HER AGAIN!" Connor barks as he is being approached by a manager.

"We can't have that here. I'm going to have to ask you to leave."

This was definitely not the spa treatment Sarah was expecting, and maybe she should have come alone after all.

"let's just go, Connor. I don't want to cause any problems."

They leave the spa, and Sarah kisses Connor and tells him she will talk with him when she gets home. Connor is trying to explain, but Sarah is upset and storms out the door. On the way home, Sarah takes a moment to think about what just happened. *Why is he so overprotective?*

As she drives around, she sees the lady who drove past her house in the black van a few weeks ago. The woman was at the post office dropping off mail in the drop off box.

"Hey… you were outside my home a few weeks ago. I wanted to talk to you."

The woman rushes to her van and doesn't say a word.

"Heyyy... who are you, and what do you want?" Sarah quizzes as she gets out of her truck and walks up to the woman.

"Stop following me and stop talking to me. I have nothing to say to you.

"Wait, tell me who you are!!!!" Sarah is yelling at the woman as she drives off.

This was strange, things are really starting to get creepy, and Sarah doesn't have a clue what's going on. Her kids are still away for camp, and she needs to find some time to pamper herself. In the meantime, and with all the crazy things happening lately, she definitely needs to have some fun and let her hair down. She stops by the coffee shop and grabs some coffee to calm her nerves.

A gentleman stops by and stares at her. He stared for about two minutes before walking up to her saying, "Excuse me, miss. I couldn't help but notice you were sitting alone. Are you expecting anyone?"

"No, I'm actually getting some me time away from the world." Sarah definitely needed this time to herself.

"So you won't mind me joining you?" he says as he pulls up a chair.

"Well, I kind of... never mind, why not," Sarah says as she is frustrated and decides not to make a big deal out of it, and besides, right now, she could use the company.

"You're not from around here. Where are you from?"

"I'm from South Carolina. I just moved here with my children. We came here to be closer to my best friend. She has been here for years and wanted us to come and get a new start."

The guy just stares at Sarah, wanting more than a conversation.

"How about we go out to dinner sometime? I'm sure I can do a lot of things to you—"

"Excuse me. I think you need to leave," Sarah interrupts.

"Oh, come on now. You know you like it. Why don't we get up from here and head back to my place?" He gets up out of his chair and grabs Sarah by the arms.

"Get your hands off me! I'm not going anywhere with you. You're psycho!"

Suddenly, Connor comes out of nowhere and punches the guy, and knocks him down to the floor.

"CONNOR STOP! STOP! YOU'RE GOING TO KILL HIM!" Sarah yells.

Connor beats the man so severely until an employee of the place breaks it up. The guy lays on the ground bleeding, holding his nose, Connor is in a rage, and he finally tries to explain why he was here in the first place

"I was driving by and noticed your car, so I stopped. I'm glad I did because there's no telling what that creep would have if I hadn't shown up."

"Thank you so much, Connor. I'm glad you showed up as well."

Sarah hugged him but has a look on her face as if it were creepy that he even popped up, especially after what just happened at the spa.

"Let's go, I'm taking you to dinner, and we're going to forget all about this," Connor says as he grabs her coffee and walks out the door.

\* \* \*

She and Connor went to this lovely restaurant and ate. They ordered salmon, which was Sarah's favorite.

"This is just what I needed. It's been a rough week, or should I say months. I'm sure it has been, but we are going to get through this, Sarah, you and me."

Maybe this isn't what Sarah needs, but she's definitely sticking by Connor through all of his crazy ways. This is the first time in a long time that a man pays attention to her and really wants to be with her. Connor may be acting strange, but he's definitely showing that he wants to be with Sarah.

\* \* \*

Later that night, Sarah watches television, and suddenly she hears a knock on the patio door. *This was strange. Why would anyone be at the patio door at this time of night?* When she opened the door, no one was there. There was a note attached to the door. It read: *7101 Reign Road.*

*What did this mean?* Sarah wondered.

It was an address, but from who and why was it attached to Sarah's door? Sarah grabs the note and goes back into the house. She put the note in her purse and calls Valerie.

"Hey, sorry to wake you." Can you talk?"

"Sure. What's wrong? "I just received a note on my patio door, and it was an address written on it."

"What? What's going on over there?"

"I'm not sure, someone knocked on the patio door, and when I went to see who it was, no one was there but this note attached on the door."

"Wow! That's strange. You need security cameras installed tomorrow. Things are getting strange."

"I agree. I'm just not sure what's going on around here. I put the note in my purse, and I'm going to go to that address in the morning."

"You want me to go with you?"

"No, I'll be fine. I got my Taser with me."

Sarah goes to bed but can't help but think about what the address means. This was definitely strange.

# Chapter 5: Things Start To Heat Up

The next morning Sarah leaves the house and puts the address in her GPS and follows it. The location was an hour away. As she hit closer to the address, she starts to shake.

"Why am I shaking? Pull it together, Sarah," she encourages herself. She's never done anything like this before.

Sarah pulls up to this abandoned house. This house looks old, rusty, and looks like no one hasn't lived there in years. *Why would someone send me this address to this house?* Sarah thought to herself. She gets out of the car and walks up to the house. Looking in the windows, she saw nothing, so she decides to go around back. She got to the back of the house and began to turn the doorknob when suddenly Valerie comes from around the corner.

"SARAH... wait!"

"Valerie? What are you doing here?"

"I followed you. I knew you were too proud to ask me to come, so I came anyway. Thank me later.

"You're definitely my partner in crime."

Valerie and Sarah go inside the house. It seemed as if no one had been inside for years. "My God, it stinks," Sarah voices as she puts her hands over her mouth.

"What is that smell?" Valerie asks as she walks closer to a closed closet door.

"I think we should go," Valerie suggests.

"I agree, " says Sarah. They leave the house and follow each other back home.

*That was strange...* Sarah thought to herself. She thinks about everything that has been going on so far and thought to herself... *what is going on here?*

Sara gets home and turns on the television. *God's Not Dead 2* is showing, and she notices a guy she met while visiting Atlanta one weekend for a film festival.

"Hey, that's Chris," Sarah voices. She calls Valerie.

"Hey, Val, remember the guy we met last year in Atlanta at the film festival? The actor Chris?"

"Yes, I remember him."

"I just saw him on television. I'm watching *Gods Not Dead 2*, and I noticed him sitting apart of the jury in the courtroom scene."

"Wow! that's amazing!"

"Yes, it is. I told him that he would be on TV someday."

*** *** ***

The next morning Sarah makes a quick run to the store. She's on the cereal aisle, and as she grabs a box of cereal, the strange lady approaches her again.

"Hey, I come in peace."

"Who are you, and what do you want?"

"My name is Kathy. I've been watching you for some time now, and I just can't do it anymore."

The strange old lady was shaking and extremely nervous.

"I'm not supposed to be talking to you. I could be in serious danger for this, but it's time that you know the truth."

"What's going on, and what are you hiding?" Sarah puts down the cereal and focuses on what the lady is saying.

"She's watching me."

"What? Who is she?" Sarah quizzes.

"She, she's dangerous. She would kill me if I told.... Get out, leave this town!" the old lady freaks out and runs out of the store.

Sarah is confused and terrified, and what just happened. Sarah forgets about the grocery and follows the woman outside.

"Hey... wait!"

"No... leave me alone! Go away! If she sees me talking to you, I'm a dead woman!"

# What She Didn't Know

"Who is she? Please tell me."

The old lady gets in her old truck and drives off fast.

Sarah is standing in the parking lot, looking shocked. "What the hell is going on?" she said aloud to herself.

She gets in her vehicle and calls Valerie.

"Valerie... something strange is going on. The old lady approached me again, and she started saying some weird stuff, and I don't know what to do. She tried to tell me something, but she was terrified.

"Okay, okay. Calm down, Sarah. Now, what did she say?" Valerie encourages.

"The lady told me she had been watching me for a while and said that she wanted to tell me the truth on why and that some woman would kill her if she told. I don't know what's going on, but I'm scared."

"Okay, calm down. This is probably some crazy lady playing some kind of game with you to scare you.'

"Tomorrow morning, I'm going to the police, and I'm going to handle this once and for all," Sarah reveals.

"I don't think it's that serious, Sarah. I mean, the police? I'm sure this woman will go away eventually," Valarie counters.

Sarah stares in a daze and disagrees, "I'm not so sure."

\* \* \*

The next day Sarah calls Connor over to the house.

"Hey, what's going on? What's wrong? You sound terrified over the phone."

"Things have been happening, and I don't know what to do about it."

"ok, calm down, now what happened?" Connor asks.

"I ran into the strange old lady again, and she was saying some crazy things."

"Yeah, you said that before—"

"No, this time is different. She said some woman basically had her to watch me and that if the woman knew she was talking to me, she would kill her. She wanted to tell me something, but she was scared."

"Okay, this is crazy, we need to go to the police.

"Yeah, that's what I said."

# Chapter 6: The Set-Up

The next morning Sarah and Valerie go to the cops. They tell them what the woman said, and they leave the station. As they walked to the car Valerie forgets that she left her jacket.

"Okay, I'll be in the car," says Sarah.

Valerie goes back into the station and speaks to the detective.

"Hey, detective, I forgot my jacket... but there is something else I wanted to speak with you about."

The detective sits Valerie down and talks with her.

"Okay, what do you want to talk about?"

"I want you to look into a Connor Gibson. he's Sarah's new boyfriend, and it's something very strange about him."

"Something like what?"

"Just look into him. Here is his information." Valerie hands the detective a piece of paper.

"Okay, I will do my best," the detective replies. As Valerie leaves the room, the detective stops her. "Hey, don't forget your jacket."

*** *** ***

Later that day, Sarah meets with Connor at his place. Connor pours her a glass of wine, and they sit on the couch to talk.

"I just don't know what's going on anymore," Sarah voices as she drinks her wine.

"Everything is going to be alright," Connor says as he leans in for a kiss.

There's a knock on the door.

"Are you expecting someone?"

"Not that I know of." Connor goes to the door. "Who is it?"

"It's the police. Come out with your hands up, or we are coming in!"

Connor opens the door, and the cops rush at him and slams him on the floor.

"Connor Gibson, you are under arrest for the murder of Alison Dickerson. You have the right to remain silent…"

As the police is taking Connor away, Sarah silently stares in disbelief.

"Sarah... this is a mistake. I promise I didn't do it!!!"

They put Connor in the back of the police car, and they take him away. Sarah just stands there not saying anything. She cannot believe what is going on right now. This can't be what she moved here for. *Murder?* she thought to herself... *couldn't be.*"

She called Valerie and lets her know what's going on.

"Valerie.... They just took Connor away."

"Who did, sweetie? Calm down. What's going on over there?"

"The police. They came and arrested Connor, saying that he under arrest for the murder of that woman who was missing. I just don't know what to do, Valerie."

"Calm down, everything is going to be okay. Where are you?"

"I'm at Connor's place."

Okay, I'm coming over right now."

Sarah quietly sits in the living room of Connor's home, shocked at what had just happened. She goes to the kitchen and get some water, and she notices a drawer was pulled out with paper piled up inside. as she pulls the drawer out, she sees a knife with blood on it. Sarah panics and walks back and forth around the kitchen.

"What? It's him! He did it!" She panics as she puts her shoes on and leaves the house.

She calls Valerie and tells her she will meet her back at the house in an hour. Sarah goes to the police station.

"Yes, some officers just arrested a friend of mine, and I need to see those officers," Sarah relays to the front desk clerk.

While she waits in the waiting room, she cries. Sarah would have never believed that Connor was a murderer.

"Miss Atkins?" the officer greets. "How can I help you?"

"Yes, I have something that might help with the case against Connor." Sarah reaches in her bag and pulls out the knife.

The officer stares at Sarah in a daze. "Where did you get that from?"

"I got it from Connor's kitchen drawer," Sarah answers.

"If you would, let me have that ma'am and get it over to the evidence room. We want to thank you so much for that. I'm sorry you have to go through this, but maybe this was best."

"You're welcome," Sarah says as she stares into space, walking away.

As she leaves out the door, she asked the officer, "How did you know my name?"

"What do you mean, ma'am?"

"Just a minute ago, you said my maiden name. I never gave you my name nor my maiden name at the house."

"Oh well, we talked with Connor as I asked him questions on the way to the station and he told us."

## What She Didn't Know

*Mmmmmm,* Sarah thought to herself. "Oh…" she says. as she leaves the station, she has a feeling that something strange is going on. *I never told Connor my maiden name.* This was very strange, and Sarah knew had to figure this out quickly.

*** *** ***

The next day she gets the kids ready for school. The kids had been back from summer camp for a few days now.

"Come on, you guys, we can't afford to be late again today," Sarah urges.

Carli runs down the stairs and says," Mommy, I'm ready."

"Okay, sweetie, where is your brother?"

"He's coming."

"Zack!!! Come on, we have to go!"

"Mom, I'm coming."

"NOW!" Sarah yells.

"Mom, are you okay? Carli wonders.

"I'm okay, sweetie. I'm just under a lot of stress."

On the way to the car, Carli says, "Mom why was Aunt Valerie over here the other day?"

"What do you mean, sweetie? She wasn't."

"Yeah, she was. She came through the back door and went into your room and looked through your purse, Carli explains.

"Did you see her?"

"Yeah, I was in my room and saw her coming through the back door. I saw from my window, then she went in your room."

"While I was out running around the block?" Where was your brother?"

"He was playing his video games."

"Well, what did she get from my purse?"

"A piece of paper...and then she left."

That was strange. Valerie was supposed to be at the gym during that time. Usually, Sarah doesn't leave the kids alone, but she had to run a mile around the block and left Zack in charge for fifteen minutes.

*I wonder what that could have been about?* Sarah thought to herself.

※ ※ ※

A few weeks past and Sarah is feeling relieved. They finally convicted Connor of Allison's murder. It all adds up, she thought. The scratch on his neck was from Allison's struggle before he killed her, the strange old woman telling her he's dangerous, the phone calls, it had made sense.

"How could I be so blind," Sarah wonders aloud as she drinks a cup of coffee while relaxing on the sofa. They sentenced him to 50 years in prison with no parole. The officers revealed that Connor wasn't his actual name. It was Peter Collins, which made even more sense. The note, a phone call, and the woman at the restaurant all mentioned that name. Sarah felt like a fool. She had gained strong feelings for Connor, not to mention having sex with him. This couldn't be karma because she's never did anyone wrong in her entire life. Maybe she will never love again, I mean, she finally lets someone in, and this happens… what now?

# Chapter 7: Behind Bars
## Connor

*I'm not sure what's going on here,* he thought to himself. *Murder? It wasn't me. What is happening to me?* Connor sits in his cell, depressed, scared, and confused. He paces back and forth, keeps calling guards for a phone call, and no one seems to allow him to make one. This was the end for him. He murdered a woman, and now his chances with Sarah are over for good.

*What could she think of me?* He thinks to himself while staring out the bars of the call. A guard finally shows up and allows Connor to make a call. The first person he calls is Sarah.

"Sarah, it's Connor. It wasn't me. You have to believe me."

Sarah doesn't say a word. She just holds the phone in disbelief for a while.

"I found the knife, Connor."

"What knife?" Connor says in confusion.

"The knife in your kitchen drawer with blood on it. The one you killed Allison with. It's over, Connor." Sarah hands up the phone before Connor could even explain himself.

Connor is lost. He's not sure what to do now. "I didn't do this!" he screamed aloud.

This had to be tough for him. He honestly believes he did not kill that woman, and someone is setting him up. Or is that what actually is happening? Is someone framing Connor for Allison's murder? If so, why? Who would want to do that to Connor? Something strange was going on.

Later that night, a guard comes to Connor's cell. "You're being set up. Get a lawyer and do not say anything to Officer Warren."

"What?" Connor says. "What's going on? Why is someone setting me up?"

The guard walks off without saying another word, and Connor is left doing some thinking to himself. *Someone is setting me up, and I'm going to get to the bottom of it. I gotta get out of here.*

## Sarah

*Maybe I shouldn't have moved here,* she thought to herself while pouring a glass of wine. She's not sure what to do next. She only came here because Valerie wanted to be closer to her and the kids and get a new life. Although it was a good idea to date again, she believed she should have done a background check on Conner first. How could this be? Everything was perfect, and she was finally starting to love again after the nasty divorce from Ethan. Maybe it was too soon to date. Perhaps she needed some time for herself and her children.

While evaluating everything that has happened, Sarah goes on a run in the neighborhood. While running, she noticed the woman outside her home a few months ago, and she immediately went over to her and decided to talk with her.

"Hey, you were at my home a few months ago…"

Before Sarah could say another word, the woman said," He didn't do it."

Sarah looks with confusion on her face.

"Who didn't do what?"

The murder… he didn't do it. It was her."

"Her? Who is her? What are you saying and what do you know about this?"

The woman doesn't say another word. She just walks off and gets in her vehicle.

Sarah is really confused at the moment. Her boyfriend has been arrested for murder, and although the evidence is all leading to him, these strange women are saying otherwise. Who is she? Not only did this woman mentioned something about a woman, but the strange old lady relayed the exact thing. Something is going on, and Sarah's about to get down to the bottom of it.

※ ※ ※

Sarah decides to take a trip to the jail where Connor is. As she walks in, she notices the awful smell. Jail was definitely a place she has never been. She asked the officer to speak with Connor Gibson. While waiting for an officer to escort her to the back, she notices an officer who came to Connor's house. It was the same officer who knew her maiden name without her even mentioned it to him.

"Hey, officer, It's Sarah," she calls out as she walks over to him.

"Yes, I remember. Why are you here?"

"I'm here to talk with Connor."

"Connor? Well, why do you want to talk to him? He did it, Sarah. We have his prints. There's nothing anyone can do now to save him.

"Well, that's why I'm here, Sarah replies, "to ask some questions."

"Questions like what?" the officer asked.

"I would prefer to speak with Connor about them," she says as she sits back down and waits for the officer to take her to the back.

"Well he's guilty, so don't go in there thinking otherwise. We got him right where we want him and don't want you or anyone else getting in the way of that.

"Excuse me?" Sarah says, but the officer walks away.

This was strange, the officer was behaving very odd, and Sarah had no idea why. She's finally being escorted to the back, and she sits down in a room and talks to Connor one-on-one.

"I didn't do this, Sarah. You have to believe me. Someone is setting me up.

"I know," Sarah replies.

"You know?"

"Yes. I think someone is out to get you. Something isn't adding up, and the officer is acting real strange. Connor, I need to ask you something. Do you know a Peter Collins?"

"What? No, who is Peter Collins?"

That's what I'm trying to figure out. The strange phone calls I've gotten was saying something about Peter Collins and the letters left on my car window, and the woman from the restaurant that night calling you Peter Collins."

"I don't know who that is."

"Connor... did you tell the officer my maiden name?"

"Your maiden name? Of course not, I never knew your maiden name.

"Connor, we have to get you out of here. They are setting you up, and I'm going to get you a lawyer. Don't talk to anyone, especially that Officer Warden, and I will do my best to get you out of here.

"Wait... did you say, Officer Warden?" Connor says as he stands up from the table with a confused look on his face."

"Yes, the officer that handled your arrest that night. He said he spoke with you, and you told him my maiden name.

"Sarah, how does he look?"

"He's chubby, maybe late 60s, blonde hair, why?"

"Sarah, I have to get out of here. He's setting me up. You have to get me out of here now."

"What's going on? How do you know him?"

Five years ago, I worked for an adoption agency. This little girl was being abused by her dad, and I had to step in and assigned the little girl to a family. Officer Warden was the little girl's dad. He blamed me for it, and now he's back for revenge.

For years now, I haven't seen him, and all of a sudden, he moves here and is trying to get back at me."

"Where did he move from?" Sarah asks.

"South Carolina, where you're from. The agency I worked for is here in Florida, but I also helped at an agency there in South Carolina before, and during that time is when the adoption took place. His little girl should be six years old now. I remember everything about her. She had a scar behind her ear, and she was the most beautiful little girl I've ever seen."

"What was the name of the adoption agency?" Sarah quizzes.

"Greater Adoption Agency."

Sarah puts her hands over her mouth and falls down into the chair.

"What's wrong? Are you okay? Connor says as he reaches over, trying to comfort her.

"That's my little girl."

"What are you talking about? What do you mean, your little girl?

"Carli..." Sarah answers. "We adopted her as a newborn. After Ethan and I had Zack, we couldn't have any more children, so we decided to adopt. That's the agency where we got her from."

"So he traced you and moved here?" Connor speculated.

"And he must have found my address as well, but why?" Sarah voices. *Why would he want Carli back after all these years?* "If he's framing you, that means he wants you in jail so that...he can come for me next."

* * *

It was time for Sarah to do some digging of her own. She goes home and make several phone calls and go online and do a little research. This wasn't making any sense. So Officer Warden's murdering these women and setting Connor up for it? And that doesn't make sense because the strange women are saying a woman is doing all of this. Everything is just confusing at this point.

Sarah had to get down to the bottom of it and fast. She sits in her chair in her living room and thinks hard about all of this. What woman could these women be talking about? This was tough to figure out what's going on, but she had to sit long and hard and think. Suddenly, she drops her glass of wine, and it shatters.

"Valerie!" Sarah announces as she slowly gets up from the chair.

Valerie's the one who knew about the adoption. She's the one who knew where Sarah was when she went to the strange house that was on the piece of paper. She also came over while Sarah was out for a run and looked through her purse. Valerie had been acting very strange, and it all adds up.

Sarah makes a call down to the station and tells the officer about Valerie. This was exceedingly difficult to do, but she couldn't just let Connor sit in jail for something he didn't do. Sarah thought to herself, *Why would Valerie murder anyone?* This still isn't adding up, but Valerie had to be at least questioned so that she could get down to the bottom of all this.

*** *** ***

They bring Valerie into the station the next day and question her. Valerie is furious and is yelling at everyone.

"Why am I here? I have done nothing wrong!"

The officers remind her that everyone is a suspect, and everyone had to be questioned.

"Whose idea was this?" Valerie demands.

"Ma'am, it was actually your friend's idea."

Valerie looks at the officer and yells, "Sarah had me dragged down here? I cannot believe this!"

*** *** ***

While they have Valerie down at the station, Sarah was home doing more research. While on the laptop, she gets a knock at the door. It was the woman who had been outside her home a few months ago.

"Why are you here?" Sarah questions to the woman.

"I'm here to help."

"What can you help me with exactly?" Sarah asks as she folds her arms.

"Let me come in, and I'll tell you."

Sarah lets the woman in, and they have a conversation. While in the middle of the conversation, Sarah gets a call from the police station.

"It's Officer Station. Ma'am, we are just informing you we have Valerie down at the station like you asked, and her story seems to check out."

"Hold on, I'm coming down," Sarah informs the officer.

She gets off the phone and tells the woman, "And you're coming with me."

What??? No... I can't."

"Yes, you are. You're going to tell me if Valerie the woman you've been talking about. I'm getting down to the bottom of this once and for all."

They leave Sarah's home and head to the station.

*** *** ***

When they walk in, the officer takes them to a room where they cannot be seen on the opposite side of the glass to identify if Valerie is the person the woman had been referring to.

Walking in on the other side of the glass, the woman immediately says, That's not her."

"What do you mean that's not her?"

"That's not the woman who has been doing all of this."

Sarah doesn't know which way to go now. She had the police bring her best friend down to the station and be humiliated, and she wasn't the woman who had done this.

"I feel awful, Sarah says. Can you guys please let Valerie go? I need to speak with her now."

As the officers are escorting Valerie out, Sarah tries to apologize to Valerie.

"I DON'T WANT TO HEAR ANYTHING!" Valerie roars with tears in her eyes. "WE`RE DONE. THIS FRIENDSHIP IS OVER!"

Sarah doesn't say a word. She just stands there as Valerie walks out of the police station. This had to be awful for Sarah. She didn't trust her best friend and even blamed her for the murder. Now she back to square one, and Connor is still in jail. The police aren't letting Connor out, even with the strange woman telling them a woman was behind all of this. They have Connors fingerprints on the knife, so that's all they can rely on at this moment.

# Chapter 8: Strange Behavior

Some things weren't adding up. Sarah had to figure out what was going on, if Connor and Valerie were innocent, who was left to blame? Sarah drives around for hours trying to think to herself. She goes to the gas station and while in line she decides to give the adoption agency a call and ask some questions. She has them to look into her file and check everything out and do a full investigation.

After being on the phone with the agency for fifteen minutes, she grabs some food for the kids and head back home. After lunch, she takes a nap. Sarah has really had a long few months and all of this was very strange to her.

*** *** ***

After her nap, she goes do some further investigating of her own, so she drops the kids off at the nanny for a few hours. She's at the library using a computer to dig up all she could on Officer Warden and his family, but she found nothing. While going to the ladies' room, she sees her landlord.

"Mrs. Greenburg, hey, how are you?"

Mrs. Greenburg looks as she had seen a ghost.

"I'm doing fine, Mrs. Harrington."

"What are you doing here?" Sarah asks.

"Oh, I love to come here to read and get some me time for myself."

"All the way from Tampa?"

Crestview was hours away from Tampa, so Sarah is confused about why Mrs. Greenburg would come all the way out here to use the computer.

"Oh, I was just visiting someone in the neighborhood. I have properties here and was doing my rounds while in the area."

"Oh, okay, well, it was nice seeing you again."

"Likewise, how is that home of yours? Are you enjoying it?"

"Yes, it's wonderful."

"Well, I have to go. I will see you soon, okay." Mrs. Greenburg then rushes off.

Sarah couldn't help but think that was strange. Mrs. Greensburg would never drive all the way out here just to use a computer. The woman hates driving!

\*\*\* \*\*\* \*\*\*

After Mrs. Greenburg's mom's death, she moves to Florida and start a new life. She's been here for about three years now, and she's immensely popular in the neighborhood. She's sold many homes around the town, and everyone seems to love her. She recently reached out to Sarah through social media, and that's how

## What She Didn't Know

she found her and sold her a home. It was extremely fast. Sarah had just gotten a divorce from Ethan, so buying a home wasn't exactly Sarah's plan at the time, but Mrs. Greenburg was so consistent about selling her a home for a reasonable price that Sarah couldn't turn down. When Mrs. Greenburg sold Sarah the house, she disappeared. She's always been a very secretive person and loved to be by herself most of the time. She had a home in Tampa that was very nice. It was a five-bedroom home with a three-car garage, a nice, beautiful pool in the backyard, and a big, lovely palm tree in front of her yard.

She never really left the house. She's been married for ten years now, but she and her husband never see each other. He was a police officer and was always on the go, so they never have alone time. This drove Mrs. Greenburg to depression. Although she looked fine on the outside, she was a mess on the inside. Her life isn't all that she puts on display to be. She has many skeletons in her closet.

* * *

Sarah is sitting out at the pool, enjoying herself and sipping on wine, when she notices a dog who was on her lawn barking and sniffing at her garden she recently grew. She goes over to scare the dog away when suddenly she sees the dog did not move an inch. Sarah grabs a shovel and tries to scare the dog while yelling at it, and the dog seems to ignore her. Finally, she hits the dog over and over with the shovel, and the dog bites her. Bleeding and screaming, she calls the police, but what's strange is that while waiting on the police, the dog is still barking at the dirt.

*What is he barking at?* Sarah thought to herself. She had started to worry, but I'm sure it was nothing. The police arrive fifteen minutes later, and the dog is still barking. They removed the dog from her backyard and made sure Sarah got her hand looked at.

"What could he be barking at?" Sarah questioned the officer.

"I'm not sure, ma'am, but whatever it was, I'm sure it's nothing.

Later that night, Sarah sits on her couch, staring outside at her garden, wondering what the dog could have been barking at. Although she wanted to go out there and do some digging, she didn't want to seem crazy.

*** *** ***

The next day she goes on a run, trying to clear her head. Connor is still in jail, Valerie is mad at her, and everything is falling apart. What could go wrong next? While running, a strange vehicle approaches her. The car is going real slow, and every time Sarah tries to speed up, the car speeds up. Finally, Sarah panics and stop.

"What is your problem?" she yells at the vehicle.

Suddenly the person in the vehicle hits the gas, trying to run Sarah down and kill her. She jumps out of the way just in time, but whoever this was wanted her dead.

*What the hell is happening?* she thought to herself. *Someone is trying to kill me.*

After talking to the police, she realized that she had no help. The cops told her there's nothing they could do because she didn't get the plate number of the vehicle. All she knew as far as the description was it was a black van with tinted windows. Police officers are never really good help. All they do is wait for something to happen before they actually do something about the situation. Sarah had to do something about this situation on her own. She had to find out who was trying to kill her and who was setting Connor up.

She went to the house and laid down on the couch trying to figure out what was going on when suddenly, she hears a knock on the door. It was the strange lady who was watching her home, the same one who she took to the police station.

"Hey, what are you doing here?' Sarah asks.

"I'm sorry to bother you. I just wanted to see how you were doing."

"I'm doing fine. Sarah then takes a deep breath. "Okay, I'm not, come in."

She invites the woman in. They have a cup of coffee and sit down on the sofa.

"Someone tried to kill me this afternoon."

"What? are you serious? who was it?"

"I'm not sure, but whoever it was, drove a black van with tinted windows.

"What? Are you serious? Could it be the woman who told me to tell you all those things about Connor?"

"Maybe so, but I'm not completely sure. It's nothing I can do now but protect myself."

"Hey, let's go take a walk at the park, get some air, and get you out of this house.

"That doesn't sound like a bad idea."

The ladies go have a girls' day out at the park, getting a whip of fresh air and just forgetting about all the crazy stuff that has been going on.

"Hey, that woman you said told you those things. Have you seen her lately?"

"No, actually, I haven't seen her in weeks. She shows up every few weeks, and then she disappears. The crazy thing is I've seen her face somewhere but not sure where," Sarah explains. "She had blonde hair, in her late 50s, drove a nice black Mercedes. I could tell the woman had money. I'm not sure who that could be, but I hope she's long gone by now," Sarah says.

As she reaches in her purse and pulls out her phone, she gets a call from Mrs. Greenburg.

"Hey, where are you?" Mrs. Greenburg asks.

"I'm at the park with a friend," Sarah answers. "Is everything okay?"

"Yes, everything is fine. I wanted to bring you the paperwork I told you about a few weeks ago. They came in this morning, so I was going to drop by."

"Oh, wow, let me get home. I will be there in about fifteen minutes."

"Ok, no problem, I have a key, so I'll just go in and wait," Mrs. Greenburg replies.

"Hey, that was my realtor. She's waiting for me. She's bringing me some important paperwork. Let's pick back up tomorrow evening and get together," Sarah relays to the woman.

"Great, sounds like a plan."

Just as she was heading to the car, Sarah gets a call from the nanny.

"Hey, the school had a gas leak, and the kids were let out early. I picked the kids up, and we are here at the house. By the way, the realtor is here."

"Yes, she's waiting for me. I'm headed there now. Just leave the kids there. I know you have another job to go to. They will be fine."

"Okay, see you later."

Sarah hangs up and heads to the car.

"Hey, I'm actually looking to buy a new home soon. Maybe you could have your realtor to give me a call," the woman suggests.

"Oh sure, as a matter of fact, here is a card, her name is Catherine Greenburg, she's excellent," Sarah explains.

As she hands the woman the card, the woman notices the photo on the front of the card.

"THAT'S HER!" she panics.

"Excuse me, who are you talking about?" Sarah quizzes.

"HER... THE WOMAN THAT'S BEEN TELLING ME TO SAY THOSE THINGS TO YOU. THAT'S HER!"

"What?"

"SHE CHANGED HER HAIR... BUT THAT IS DEFINITELY HER!!!"

In the middle of their conversation, Sarah gets a call from the adoption agency.

"Sarah Harrington, this is Pat Singleton with Greater Adoption Agency. We are here with the detectives, and we've found some vital information involving your adoption case. The files were tampered with, and the real father is Bill Warden. He's Carli's birth father, but there's more. His wife, which is Carli's birth mom, is Amanda Warden. Amanda was a mental patient at Hope Hospital.

After she killed her mother. Amanda's mom knew she wasn't able to raise Carli, so she contacted us to put Carli in the adoption system. Amanda found out and stabbed her thirty times in the chest and cut her head off. She was sentenced to life in prison, but the judge thought she was insane and ordered for her to be locked away in a mental institution for the rest of her life. She escaped three years ago and has been missing since. The detectives informed us that she's going by the name Catherine Greenburg, and they found out she's your realtor. We need you to contact the police there right away. She's considered to be armed and an extremely dangerous woman," Pat reveals.

"SHE'S AT MY HOUSE AND MY KIDS ARE THERE!" Sarah panics.

"Call the police right now, ma'am. They are in danger!"

# Chapter 9: Saving Carli

Sarah rushes home to save her children. The entire way there, she's crying and terribly upset. *Why would she do this to me?* she thought. Sarah knew it would be hard to give up a child, but years later, to come and find her was ridiculous. Sarah pulls up to the driveway and rushes into the house.

"Carli???? Zack???? Where are you?"

She went into the kitchen and found them tied in a chair with duct tape around their mouth and rope around their feet.

"Oh my god! Mommy is here!"

As she tries to untie them, Amanda comes around the corner.

"Well, well, well, you finally arrived."

"Why are you doing this, Amanda? What do you want from me?"

"I see you've done your homework. Why am I doing this? Mmmmm, let's see. I waited all my life to have kids. I finally have one, and then my bitch mother calls the adoption agency to have my child taken from me. They give her to a pretty woman who already has a kid. What about me???" she screams as she waves her gun around. "Who thought about me? Where is my happiness? She just called and requested that they take my child, and I had to get rid of her."

"What do you want?" Sarah quizzes as she stands in front of her children.

"I want my daughter back. She was never yours to begin with. She's mine, and I'm not leaving this house without her."

Carli and Zack are crying and mumbling.

"Shut up! Just shut up already! Look... I'm here to take what's mine. I don't want to hurt anyone."

"I can't let you take her. We have our rights to adopt her, and that's what we did. Your mother signed the consent form, so we did nothing wrong. Carli is ours."

NOOO! Stop saying that!!!!!! She's mine... and I'm walking out the back door with her."

As Amanda tries to move closer to grab Carli, Sarah jumps in the way, trying to stop her. "One more move, and you're dead."

"Please, don't do this. She's my baby girl!" Sarah says as she's crying.

"Well, she's mine now, so get out of my way, or I will shoot," Amanda warned.

Sarah slowly moves out of the way, and Amanda unties Carli. She grabs her and makes her walk to the backdoor with her.

"Please don't do this! Please!" Sarah pleaded.

"I'm sorry, Sarah, but a mother has to do what a mother has to do. When we leave, don't follow us or I'll kill her," Amanda threatened. She leaves the house with Carli, and Sarah starts screaming and crying.

As Sarah unties Zack, she calls the police. While waiting for the police to come, she tells Zack to go to his room and lock the door.

\*\*\* \*\*\* \*\*\*

Sarah decides to follow them. She tries to stay a few cars behind so that Amanda wouldn't see her. She almost lost her a few times, but she stayed on her tail. Wherever she's taking Carli, it's a long way out, It's almost dark, and the police finally calls.

"Sarah, it's Officer Forman. We are at your home with Zack. Where are you?

"I'm following Amanda Greenburg. She took Carli and said if I followed her, she'd kill her, but I'm staying a few cars behind, so she won't notice me."

"Do not follow her, Sarah. We have an APB out on Mrs. Greenburg's vehicle, and we are tracking her. I repeat, do not follow her. She's dangerous and could kill your daughter. Let us handle it from here. We have officers on the way following her."

"I'll have to take that chance," Sarah says as she hangs up the phone.

The vehicle Amanda was in was slowing down. They were turning into an old, abandoned house. *Why is she going here?* Sarah thought to herself. This was the house she went to after she received a piece of paper on her patio door.

Amanda turns into the yard and carries Carli into the abandoned house. Sarah parks on the street, turns out her lights, and quietly gets out of the vehicle. She peeks into the window and saw nothing, so she goes to the side of the house and looks in the window and sees Carli lying on the bedroom floor.

"OMG, Carli! Mommy is here to get you, baby," she says aloud quietly to herself.

Sarah goes around the back and tries to break into the house. Suddenly, Amanda hits her in the head with a shovel. Amanda then drags Sarah into the house and ties her up.

\*\*\*

After being out for an hour, she finally wakes up.

"Well, well, well, look who's up."

"Why are you doing this?" Sarah says.

"I told you not to follow me. Since you're here, you might as well toast to Carli coming home."

Amanda pulls out a bottle of champagne.

"Open up," Amanda orders as she stands over Sarah with the bottle.

"Noo!" Sarah says.

"I said open, you selfish bitch!"

Amanda grabs Sarah and forces her to drink.

"You're crazy!" Sarah yells. "The police are on the way!"

"No, they're not," Amanda counters.

"Yes, they are. I just called them on the way here, and they have your vehicle traced. You may as well give up now."

"I figured they would do that, which is why I purchased two of the same vehicles," Amanda discloses. "Have you ever noticed my license plate from when I first met with you in person and the license plates of the vehicle I was in that day at the library? Two different plates... and this car isn't even in my name, so the person their following is on their way out of the state right now!" Amanda sneers.

Sarah puts her head down and cries. "Why are you doing this? Please let us go!"

"Aww, why am I doing this again? I already explained that to you, Sarah. Carli is my daughter, and when she wakes up, we will be in New Mexico enjoying our new life, and you... well, you'll be dead."

## What She Didn't Know

Amanda puts the tape back over Sarah's mouth.

"Now, I have some errands to run. When I get back, you will see the other side of eternity." Amanda leaves the house.

While she's gone, Sarah tries to escape. At first, she sits there and cries of disbelief. After a while, She tries to get out of the chair but struggles to do so, so she tries to make the chair fall so that it can break, and she could get loose. She tries for fifteen minutes and can't seem to get it. She sits there screaming for help, but she's miles from anyone, and no one can hear her. Sarah keeps trying to get loose, and finally, she manages to grab the kitchen knife that was on the table in front of her, pulls it behind her hands, and cuts the rope.

After several minutes, she finally breaks free. She runs and checks on Carli, but she's still sleeping. Sarah notices that her phone is on the kitchen table, so she calls the police and tells them everything.

While waiting on the police, Carli wakes up, and she sees her mom. "Mommy!"

"Carli, baby, I'm here to get you."

Sarah and Carli escape from the backdoor and runs into the woods. While trying to find help, she sees a highway. They get on the highway, and Sarah stops the first car she sees.

"Helpppp! Stop! We need your help!" she yells.

Are you guys okay?" the young man asks.

"No, someone is trying to kill us, and we need help!"

"Get in. There is a police station down the road."

"I have already called the police. They are on the way." Sarah reveals as she gets in the car.

"Ok, good. Let's wait on them."

Before Sarah could say another word, Amanda shoots the guy's front windshield.

"Get out of the car," Amanda orders.

"Okay, just relax," Sarah says.

"Relax? You want me to relax? My sister and I have suffered for years because of your mistake. We planned this from the beginning, and if you think you're going to ruin this for me this time, you're out of your mind. say goodbye."

Amanda's about to shoot Sarah when suddenly the cops show up.

"You called the cops... you stupid bitch!!!!!" Amanda puts the gun up to her own head. "If Carli can't live with me, she's going to have to live without me!"

"Put the gun down!" the officers ordered.

Amanda slowly puts the gun down, and the officers placed her in handcuffs.... You won't get away with this! You hear me!

# What She Didn't Know

You won't get away!!! Amanda screams while being placed in the police car.

"Are you okay, ma'am?" the officer asks.

"Yes, I'm fine now."

All of this was unbelievable. Her realtor? Sarah would have never thought. This was like a dream, or more like a nightmare. How could this happen?

*** *** ***

Weeks have passed, and everything was back to normal. They had Amanda in jail facing a life sentence, Connor was released from jail, they found the body of Allison Dickerson at the abandoned house, and Officer Warden was also arrested for tampering with an investigation and making a false arrest.

While in jail, Amanda has a visitor. The guard sits her at the table, handcuffed, waiting on her visitor to arrive. *Who could this be?* she thought. The visitor finally walks into the room, and it's her sister.

"Don't worry, lil sis. I just came to tell you that they are gonna pay. I'm going to make Sarah's life a living hell," her sister vows as she turns back around and begins to leave the room. Amanda stands up and says, "Thanks, VALERIE. Now go and bring Carli home."

# To Be Continued

Made in the USA
Columbia, SC
13 October 2024